To my dear grandchildren, and in memory of Suzie-B.E.C.
To my sweet daughters-R.M.

yonderhomepublishing.com

Library of Congress Control Number: 2021908717
ISBN: 978-1-954701-01-4
First paperback edition: June, 2021
10 9 8 7 6 5 4 3 2 • Printed in USA

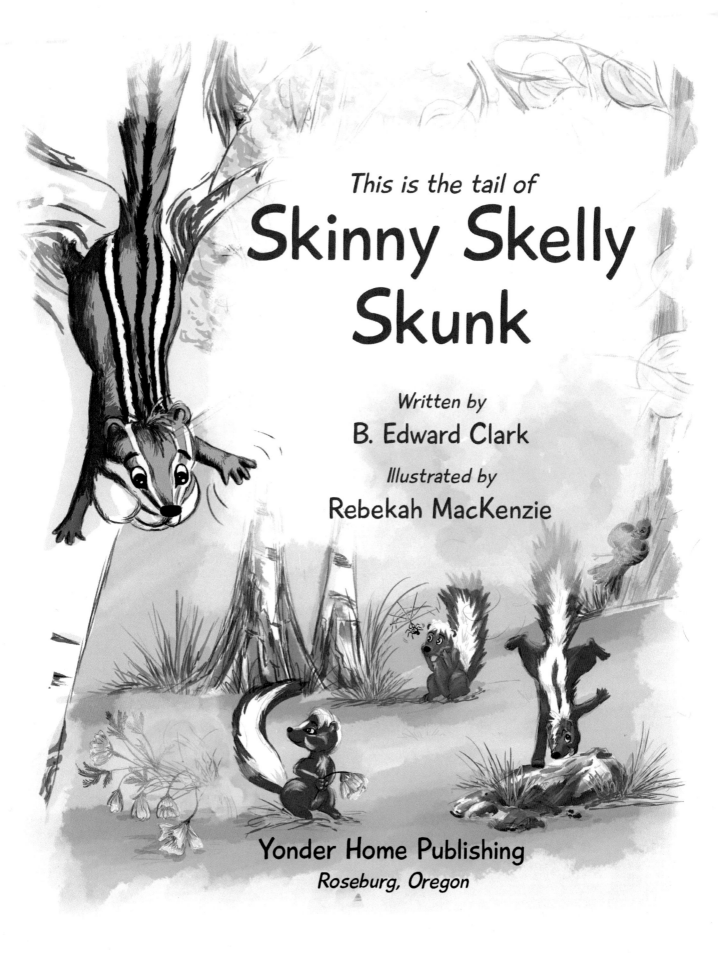

This is the tail of
Skinny Skelly Skunk

Written by
B. Edward Clark

Illustrated by
Rebekah MacKenzie

Yonder Home Publishing
Roseburg, Oregon

Newborn baby munks
with their eyes shut tight,
lie snuggled with their family
on a windy, stormy night.

Newborn baby skunks
with their little tiny peepers
closed in dreamy bliss
midst a family of sleepers.

Family mix-ups sometimes happen
when the wind is howlin'
and the thunder's clappin'!!

At last the storm is over
and the babies now can see
the wild and wondrous world that waits
beneath the canopy.

Call him, "Skinny Skelly Skunk"
'cause he's a tiny little critter;
he's a puny little punk
and the runt of all the litter!

Skinny Skelly Skunk
climbs the rocks and
trees with ease,
but the stinky stanky skunks
would only fall and
scrape their knees.

Skinny Skelly Skunk
and all the stinky stanky clan
just a playin' and a sprayin'
in every way they can.

But Skinny Skelly Skunk
has no icky sicky sprayer
though he wishes that he had one
being chased by grizzly be-ar!

Skinny Skelly Skunk
didn't stink, didn't smell,
and he wondered if the other
stinky stanky skunks could tell?

Skinny Skelly isn't smelly!?

Skinny Skelly Skunk
has a tail not so fluffy
as the stinky stanky skunks
with their tails so nice and puffy.

Stinky stanky skunks
with their stripes so bold and bright,
you can see them in the day;
you can see them in the night.

But Skinny Skelly Skunk
with his stripes so mild and meek
means that Skinny Skelly Skunk
always wins at hide 'n seek.

Skinny Skelly Skunk
with his chubby,
pouchy cheeks...

Stinky stanky skunks
whose entire bodies reek!

Skinny Skelly isn't smelly!?

Stinky stanky skunks
grow as large as Kitty Cat,
but Skinny Skelly Skunk
is no bigger than a bat.

Skinny Skelly Skunk
so petite and very small
is a thinkin' that he might
not even be a skunk at all!

Where's my puffy tail and fur
so shiny black and white?

Somethin's missing!
Somethin's wrong!
Can someone make it right?

Just then there was a chippin'
and a chatterin' behind;
so Skinny Skelly turned around
to see what he would find...

A group of rodents shouting,
"IS IT HIM? CAN IT BE?
Is that our Mini Mani Munk there
sittin' by the tree?"

Skinny Skelly knew at once
these chipmunks were his kin.
They picked him up
and took him home
and there they let him in.

What? My name's not Skinny Skelly?
No! It's Mini Mani Munk!

But in his heart
he'll always be a
stinky, stanky, skunk.

Made in the USA
Monee, IL
05 April 2022

94168668R10021